To my mom, I love you —J.A.

To my maman, who gave me the life I can live as a picture-book artist —R.J.B.

THIS IS A BORZOI BOOK PUBLISHED BY ALFRED A. KNOPF

Library of Congress Cataloging-in-Publication Data
Names: Arena, Jen, author. | Jomepour Bell, Rahele, illustrator. | Title: Give / Jen Arena, Rahele Jomepour Bell.
Description: First edition. | New York: Alfred A. Knopf, 2023. | "This is a Borzoi book" | Audience: Ages 4–8
Summary: "A group of kids learn about the act of giving all kinds of things, from scarves to a hug."—Provided by publisher.
Identifiers: LCCN 2021042252 (print) | LCCN 2021042253 (ebook) | ISBN 978-1-5247-1499-4 (hardcover)
ISBN 978-1-5247-1448-2 (library binding) | ISBN 978-1-5247-1449-9 (ebook)
Subjects: LCSH: Generosity—Juvenile literature. | CYAC: Generosity. | LCGFT: Picture books.
Classification: LCC BJ1533.G4 A68 2023 (print) | LCC BJ1533.G4 (ebook) | DDC 179/.9—dc23

The text of this book is set in 20-point Grange Rough.
The illustrations were created using oil paint on Arches paper, layered and modified in Photoshop.
Hand-lettered title by David Coulson. Book design by Martha M. Rago.

MANUFACTURED IN CHINA
10 9 8 7 6 5 4 3 2 1
First Edition

Jen Arena Rahele Jomepour Bell

GIVE

Alfred A. Knopf
New York

Sometimes
bad things happen.

Give what you have.

Sometimes
we get cold.

Give warmth.

Sometimes
something breaks.

Give
something new.

Sometimes
we forget.

Give if you remember.

Sometimes we make a mess.

Give a hand.

Sometimes we have less.

Give more.

Sometimes we're lonely.

Give friendship.

Sometimes we feel hurt.

Give comfort.

Sometimes
things are
out of reach.

Give help.

Sometimes
we are left out.

Give a piece of yourself.

The good you do comes back to you.